The Promise
MEGAN REBEKAH CUPIT

Greatest Stories Ever Told ® • Selmer, Tennessee

THE PROMISE

Megan Rebekah Cupit

ISBN, print edition: 978-09960559-1-8
ISBN, kindle edition: 978-0-9960559-2-5

Cover design by: E. Pavao
Illustrations by: Emily Person

Published by:

Greatest Stories Ever Told
P.O. Box 307
Selmer, TN 38375

731-645-0106

admin@christian-history.org
http://www.GSETpublishing.com

"𝔥𝔦𝔰𝔱𝔬𝔯𝔶 𝔦𝔰, 𝔟𝔶 𝔡𝔢𝔣𝔦𝔫𝔦𝔱𝔦𝔬𝔫, 𝔱𝔥𝔢 𝔪𝔬𝔰𝔱 𝔢𝔵𝔠𝔦𝔱𝔦𝔫𝔤 𝔰𝔱𝔬𝔯𝔦𝔢𝔰 𝔞𝔫𝔡 𝔦𝔫𝔱𝔢𝔯𝔢𝔰𝔱𝔦𝔫𝔤 𝔣𝔞𝔠𝔱𝔰 𝔬𝔣 𝔞𝔩𝔩 𝔱𝔦𝔪𝔢."

Copyright © 2014 by Megan Rebekah Cupit. All rights reserved.

Part One | Promised

The people who walk in darkness will see a great light;
Those who live in a dark land, the light will shine on them
...
For a child will be born to us, a son will be given to us;
And the government will rest on His shoulders;
And His name will be called Wonderful Counselor, Mighty God,
Eternal Father, Prince of Peace.
There will be no end to the increase of His government or of peace.
--Isaiah 9:2,6-7 (NASB)

I have never forgotten this promise. Someday, somehow—a child would change the world. He would snuff out the darkness in our world and bring us light ... the promise of hope.

As I sat with my mother and sister at the synagogue and listened to the rabbi, I felt these words seep into my heart. I had no idea how much they would change my life.

What would that be like? To live in a kingdom ruled by the Prince of Peace? Our small village of Nazareth was full of unrest, trapped under the black cloud of Rome's power. There was nothing peaceful about the way we were forced to live.

But this promise, the promise of peace and light, was spoken long ago by the prophet Isaiah, speaking for the

Lord. *If God said we would have peace, why is the world so dark? Why can't He come to us now?*

"Mary." My mother's whisper broke into my thoughts. "It is time to leave."

As I stepped out of the synagogue with my mother, my sister Leah, and the other women, I caught the sound of a man's voice. "He is coming! Our Messiah is coming!" The man didn't appear to be talking to anyone in particular, but his voice was loud, and I could see a crowd forming around him on the street corner. "There will be a new King in the land of Israel. He will reign as King, act wisely, and bring justice and righteousness in the land."

There it was again: the promise of hope.

I walked closer to the man. "In His days Judah will be saved, and Israel will be secure." The man had long, unkempt hair, and wore a dirty, tattered garment. But there was a light in his eyes that made something obvious: this man knew the true King ... the One who would bring the promise to life.

"And our new King—He will be called by this name: 'The Lord our righteousness,' and—"[1]

Suddenly his words were drowned out. A group of Roman soldiers rounded the corner and grabbed the man's arms. Even as they dragged him down the street, he didn't stop talking to the people. I couldn't hear his words because the soldiers were shouting over him, but I saw his lips moving.

---

[1] Jeremiah 23:6

Then he was gone; probably on his way to prison, or, more likely, execution.

I heard the doors of the synagogue open again, and then my brother Benjamin bumped my elbow. He watched as the crowd of listeners slipped away from the corner, watching over their shoulders to make sure no more soldiers were coming. "What happened?"

I sighed. "There was a man over there. He was telling the prophecy about the new King who would save us."

"What? Did they arrest him?"

I nodded. Benjamin's jaw tightened. I saw his dark eyes spark.

"Those no-good Roman—"

"Benjamin!" My mother appeared behind us. "Keep your voice down." Her voice was a harsh whisper. "Do you want to end up like Asher?"

Asher. My older brother. A zealot who believed that Rome was nothing but evil. He had been crucified by the Romans just the year before, after getting into a fight with a soldier.

Benjamin looked at the ground. Asher had been his hero. I watched him as he walked off. He was so young, only fourteen—two years younger than me. Unless something changed, Benjamin's life could end just as Asher's had.

This is not the way life is supposed to be.

We were quiet as we walked back to our home, my father leading the donkey that my mother sat on. I could not stop thinking about that peace, the peace that our God had promised. *Oh Lord, how our world could change if we were given only a touch of that peace.*

The next day, I gathered my neighbor's goats and brought them to graze in the hills, the same way I did almost every morning. I loved being a shepherdess. I loved the quiet and stillness that I found when I was alone. And being in the hills also gave me an excuse to walk past the rabbi's house on the way home, which meant I might get a chance to see Gideon, the rabbi's son.

Gideon was three years older than me. I had known him all my life, and he seemed to be the only boy who had ever seen me as more than just another girl from a poor family. I had a feeling ... someday, he might choose me as his wife. Someday. Maybe.

Just when the sun was starting to go down, I led my flock back to my neighbor's home and shut them in their pen. The man met me at the gate and slipped a coin into my hand. I thanked him, then walked down the road that led to the center of town. I unwrapped my head scarf as I went, letting the summer wind lift my curly hair off my damp neck and blow the dust off my clothes. It felt so good. I closed my eyes.

"Hello, Mary." My eyes flew open, and I saw Gideon standing a few feet from me, a smile in his green eyes.

I smiled back at him. "Hello, Gideon." I smoothed my scarf back over my hair, hoping I didn't have dirt from the pastures smudged on my face.

He turned to walk next to me. "So ... you have business in the village today?" I asked, mostly just to fill the quiet space.

"My father needed me to take a message to one of Joseph's men."

I thought for a second. "You mean Joseph the carpenter?" I had heard my father saying something about him the day before.

"Are there any other people named Joseph around here?" he asked me with a laugh. I kicked a pebble at him. He laughed again.

"Mary!" One of my neighbor's daughters came rushing around the corner, and Gideon quickly stepped away from me. "Your mother said to come get you! There's someone who wants to see you."

I was puzzled. No one had ever come to my house just to see me. "Who is it?"

The girl grabbed my hand. "I don't know, just hurry!" She giggled as we ran towards my house and the wind tried to pull my scarf off again.

I slowed to a walk and eased the door open. My mother rushed to meet me and almost pushed me up the stairs to the loft of our two-room house. I caught a glimpse of my father sitting at a table across from a man I vaguely recognized.

"Who is that?" I whispered.

My mother couldn't stop smiling. "It's Joseph! He's here to see *you*."

Me? I couldn't imagine why a man I barely knew would be here, asking for me. *Unless...* I felt my heart drop into my stomach as a possibility came into my mind. *But no ... he's never even talked to me. And he must be ten years older.*

My mother opened a trunk and found me a clean dress. "Put this on, and wash your face. He's waiting." She grinned as she went back downstairs.

I felt my heart starting to speed up. *Is Joseph here to propose marriage*? Everything my mother was doing seemed to point to that. She would be thrilled to see me betrothed ... to have one less portion of food to scrape out of my father's meager earnings. And I could see why she would think Joseph would be a good husband for me. He was a carpenter. He had a big house that she thought I would be happy in. And he didn't have a high position in our village, so if he married a poor girl, it would be of no consequence.

But my mother had forgotten something.

Me.

I loved Gideon—at least I thought I *could* love him. He was almost my age. He was smart and handsome and he made me laugh. And I thought ... maybe ... he might even like me. To agree to marry another man would mean throwing all of that away.

I walked to the washbowl in a daze. I splashed cold water on my face and exchanged my dusty clothes for the dress my mother had found me.

I didn't want to go downstairs, but I had no choice. There was nowhere else to go.

I walked down the stairs, dreading every creaking step.

There was a moment of awkward silence as everyone looked at me. Then my father cleared his throat. "This is Joseph. He will be your husband."

I didn't know what to say. All my words seemed to stick in my throat.

Joseph got to his feet and took my hand. His fingers were rough from years of work. But when I looked into his eyes, I was surprised at what I found there. He had kind, deep, brown eyes. This close, he seemed a little younger than when I had seen him before, more tender somehow. A strange feeling made its way into the pit of my stomach.

My father handed a goblet to Joseph, and he drank from it. Then he put it in my hand.

The wine glistened red in the dying light, but I only saw a blur as I stared at the cup. I knew what it signified. I knew I wasn't ready for this—to be tied to a man I barely knew.

My mother bumped my elbow, still smiling. I looked at her, looked at Joseph, looked at the floor for a long moment. My mother nudged me again, and motioned for me to drink.

I wasn't even getting a chance to make up my own mind. No matter how I felt about anyone else, this was my life now.

Trembling, I lifted the goblet to my lips and took a tiny sip.

My father was saying something about how the law told us we were to be as husband and wife now, but that we couldn't live together for a year. His words tried to break through the haze in my mind. Not until Joseph reached for my other hand did I realize what I had just done.

"I … I have to go," I said, pulling away and bolting out of the room. My mother called after me, but I ignored her.

I struggled during those next few days. I talked with my older sister a lot while we worked around the house. Leah reminded me that Joseph was a good man; that he came from a good family. Apparently he was even descended from King David, just as we were. She told me that he was one of the most trustworthy men in the village and wonderful with children.

What Leah told me seemed to confirm what I had seen in Joseph's eyes. I knew that I was marrying a man with strong arms and strong character, and someday I'd probably be able to be happy with him. Somewhere in those few days, I stopped inwardly fighting the decision my parents had made for me. What might have been was behind me, and that's the way it was supposed to be.

After that day, I came home from the fields on a path that didn't take me past the rabbi's house. One of those walks changed my life forever.

That day was a day just like any other. At least, it seemed that way. The skies were very still in Nazareth, with not even a hint of wind.

Then … everything changed.

Out of nowhere, a strong wind gusted across my path. Startled, I grabbed a tree branch, fighting to keep my balance.

Then he was in front of me—a man in a robe that was the purest white I had ever seen. He smiled at me, and somehow it seemed like he had known me my whole life.

"Rejoice, highly favored one, the Lord is with you."

What? Highly favored ... the Lord ... what? How does he even know me? I must have looked confused. This man—who hadn't even introduced himself before he started telling me this—was starting to scare me. His robe shone brighter than anything I had ever seen, making my head spin as I struggled to see. I tried to back away. Instead, my heel caught on something and I fell to the ground.

Instantly, the man was at my side, reaching out a strong hand and bringing me to my feet. "Do not be afraid, Mary, for you have found favor with God."

Somehow, in that moment, I realized what was happening. This was no ordinary man.

This was an angel. And he was talking to *me*.

"You will conceive in your womb. You will have a Son, and you will name Him Jesus. He will be great, and will be called the Son of the Highest; and the Lord God will give Him the throne of His father David. And He will reign over Jacob's house forever, and His kingdom will never end."

I couldn't even think. His words didn't seem to make any sense. God's Son—our true king—being born as a baby ... through *me*? Me? A simple shepherd girl? A *virgin*? I felt dizzy with the idea, but I asked him anyway. "Sir, how can that be? I've never been with a man."

He put his huge hands on my shoulders and looked straight into my eyes. "The Holy Spirit. He will come upon you, and His power will cover you. This holy child that will be born will be God's own Son."

I just stared at him for a moment. The Prince of Peace ... the Son of God that had been promised to us ... was it possible that God was using me to bring Him to earth?

The man must have seen the struggle going on in my mind. But he just kept talking.

"Your relative, Elizabeth; she will soon have a son, even in her old age. This is her sixth month, even though she was called barren."

Elizabeth? Pregnant? My cousin Elizabeth and her husband had always wanted a son ... but they were far past the age of having children.

The man—the angel—waited for me to look at him. Then, putting meaning behind every word, he spoke. "*Nothing will be impossible for God.*"

I looked at him for a moment. I could see in his eyes that he *was* telling me the truth—that Elizabeth was having a baby, and that somehow, God would work in me. *I will be the mother of God's Son!*

I knelt down in front of him. "I am the servant of the Lord. Let it be to me just as you say."

No matter what the circumstances. Even if this journey brought unanswerable questions and incredible pain.

If God wanted to use me ... I was His.

The Promise

Part Two | Blessed

It took me a few minutes to realize that the wind had stopped and the angel was gone. I was still sitting there on the ground, head bowed. I couldn't believe what had just happened.

I'm having a baby. I still couldn't believe that of all the girls on His earth, the Lord had chosen me to be the mother of His Son; to fulfill a prophecy that our people had long been looking forward to. The impossibility of it felt like a dream, but I knew in my heart that I could never have imagined what had just happened to me.

Then another thought hit me. *Wait ... I'm* pregnant *... I'm engaged, and I'm pregnant!*

They would never believe. My parents, Joseph, the townspeople ... they would never believe that God Himself had given me a child. This would look like sin—like fornication that was usually punished severely.

It was usually punished by death.

I shakily got to my feet and numbly walked as fast as I could towards my home. I would tell my sister, my closest friend. She would know what to do.

Thankfully, Leah was the only one at home. She sat in the corner with a sandal in her hand, stitching the worn leather strap yet again. She looked up, startled, as I burst into the room.

"Mary. What's going on?"

"I … need to tell you something. Not here." I didn't want to risk my mother coming in while I told Leah what had happened.

She got up and followed me to the stable behind our house. We wouldn't be overheard here. She leaned against the sagging wall, waiting.

I took a deep breath. "I saw an angel. On the way home."

She looked at me hard. "An angel? Here?"

"Yes. He told me that … I would …" The words sounded strange even in my own mind, but finally I blurted them out. "I'm the virgin, Leah! The virgin from the Messiah prophecy."

"You mean … you …"

"He told me I will have a son. And the child will be our new King." Leah was staring at the ground, no doubt trying to process what I was telling her. I moved closer, touching her shoulder. "It's happening, Leah. It's finally happening. To us, in Nazareth."

Leah finally looked back up at me. "So you're … *pregnant*?"

It still hadn't fully hit me. I nodded slowly. "That's what he said."

"How do you know that he was really telling you the truth?" She wasn't doubting me. She was just being practical Leah, making sure someone wasn't telling us some crazy story. Even if it felt like a crazy story.

"He was an *angel*. I mean … I know that was not just a man talking to me, Leah. I can't really describe it."

I didn't even know what to think, what to feel about what the angel had told me. I was thrilled that God had somehow chosen me. I was also afraid of what the people would do to me—a pregnant, unmarried girl. I was amazed that the Messiah really was coming, in *my lifetime*; and I was scared of the unknown ahead of me. So much unknown.

I saw in Leah's eyes that she understood. She believed me.

She wrapped her arms around me. "God chose you."

"I don't have any idea why," I said into her shoulder. We stood together for a few minutes, not saying anything. Then I pulled back.

"What will we do when everyone finds out?"

Her steady eyes met mine. She was always the rock I could cling to even when the world seemed to spin around me. *Thank you, Lord, for my sister.*

"God knows what He's doing. If you're to be the mother of our Messiah, He has a plan for you." Leah had always been the strong one. She was so sure now, and I wanted to believe her so badly.

"But the laws? Joseph?"

She put a finger on my lips, smiling. "Mary, whatever else happens, God's plan is *going to happen.* The Messiah is coming through you. God will protect you, I'm sure of it."

I felt a little of her strength seep into my heart. If our Lord could work a miracle, giving a child to a girl who had never been with a man, surely He could protect me until the child was born.

Then I remembered the other miracle. "Elizabeth and Zacharias are having a baby too."

"*What?*"

I laughed, breathless. It really was unbelievable. "The angel told me. They're finally having the son they've waited for all these years."

Leah shook her head, amazed. "Nothing will be impossible with God." She couldn't have known that those were exactly the words the angel had used, but somehow the connection made it sink in a little more. *Nothing is impossible with God.*

He *would* fulfill His promise.

"You should go see them!" Leah broke into my thoughts. "You should go to Elizabeth. That would give you a little more time to come up with the way to tell everyone about this."

"But I haven't seen them in years. And how would I even get there?" Elizabeth and Zacharias lived twenty miles away, farther than I could ever walk on my own.

"I heard one of the women talking about her family going that way. They're leaving soon, though. Tomorrow, I think. You'd have to ask Father."

I really did want to see Elizabeth. I wondered if she'd even remember me, especially since I no longer looked like the little girl I had been the last time I had seen her. But I longed to see God working the impossible in another life. And I wasn't sure I was prepared to face whatever would happen when people found out about my pregnancy.

I would go to Elizabeth and Zacharias.

When we all ate together that night, I got the chance to talk to my father. My heart pounded as I waited for him to come sit down. He blessed the food, and we all were quiet as we ate.

"I'd like to go see Elizabeth." I broke the silence. My voice sounded too loud in my own ears.

My mother looked at me funny. "You mean my cousin Elizabeth? It's been so long since you've seen her."

"The harvest will be here sooner than we know." My father didn't give me a chance to reply. "We will need everyone here to help."

I swallowed. This was my only chance to change my father's mind. A no was a no, and that would be final. It would truly be a miracle if my stern father allowed me to leave. *But then, all kinds of miracles are happening today.*

"I don't need to stay for a long time. Maybe two months, maybe three. I only wish to see Elizabeth."

"For what reason?" my father asked me absently.

I bit the inside of my cheek. "I heard today that Zacharias and Elizabeth are having a child." No use lying to my parents. They'd find out eventually anyway.

"A *child?*" My mother leaned towards me, her eyes intent on mine. "But she is ... she is past the age."

I shook my head, smiling. "The Lord is working. I want to see her."

My father finally turned to me, seeming to focus for the first time. "How would you get there?" He didn't even seem to recognize the impossibility of Elizabeth's pregnancy. I looked at my sister, feeling a blossom of hope open in my heart.

"I've heard that Seth's family is going that way," Leah said. "They're leaving tomorrow afternoon. They will be back before the harvest."

My father took a bite of bread, thinking. Then he finally looked at me. "If Elizabeth truly is having a child, you should be there to give her our congratulations. And I'm sure you can be of some help to her." I saw the corner of his mouth crook up into a smile. "You may go with Seth, Mary."

That night, as I gathered what I would need for the trip, Leah found me in the loft. "Before you go…I think you should talk to Joseph." Her voice was a whisper, covered by the sound of my brother and father arguing in the room below.

"Why?" I whispered back. He was the last person I wanted to face at that moment.

Leah seemed to search for words, pausing for a moment. "I think…I think he truly loves you. I've seen him watching you when we go to the synagogue and when you pass his shop. I saw the look in his eyes when you let him take your hand."

This was a new perspective. Maybe Joseph truly cared for me, as more than just a girl to make his meals and have his children. Maybe that was the tenderness I had seen in his eyes the day he came to our house. Maybe the only reason I never noticed it is because I had never thought of *him* that way.

Leah took my hands in her own. "I think you should tell him. I think he might understand. And if he really trusts you—if he believes what the angel told you—then that might be part of how God will protect you."

I couldn't even picture myself telling Joseph that I was carrying a baby. Especially if he really did love me, as strange as that seemed. But somehow, I felt myself aching for him to believe me. And Leah had been right many times before.

"I'll think on it," I said, squeezing Leah's hand and trying to smile.

I didn't sleep well that night, but by dawn the next morning I had decided to go to Joseph. He would know about this baby sooner or later, and it seemed that if I told him before it was glaringly obvious, he might be more likely to trust me.

I had never gone into Joseph's shop before, but I knew where it was. I wrapped some fresh bread in a cloth. At least that would be an excuse for going to see my betrothed.

Joseph was surprised to see me, to say the least. Even at the early hour, he was already covered in sawdust. He brushed his hands on his carpenter's apron as he came to me, looking like he didn't know whether to keep his distance or wrap me in his arms.

"Hello, Mary," he said, eyes warm, but uncertain.

I held the warm bundle out in front of me. "I just made bread. This one's for you."

He thanked me, and then a thick silence filled the space between us. I looked around. No customers were waiting for him. "Do you have time to talk?"

Joseph led me to a pair of stools, motioning for me to sit. Taking a deep breath, I poured out the entire story to him. When I stopped, he didn't look at me.

I sat there, noticing that my hands were shaking. My heart pounded. I hadn't realized how much I cared about what he thought until that moment.

He looked up. Doubt clouded his eyes. For a long time, he didn't say anything. Then he finally spoke.

"We are engaged, Mary." He looked away from me again, staring out the window. "You ... when you drank the cup ... you were saying you'd wait for me for a year." He wouldn't meet my eyes. "I just ... I don't know." He was defeated, even hurt. I could hear it in his voice. He got up and left the room, leaving me sitting there alone, wondering what had just happened.

He didn't believe me.

It hurt to know that the one man I had entrusted with my secret had rejected it ... had rejected me. It wasn't really a surprise. But it hurt. And it was just another thing to wonder about. Would Joseph turn me in? Would I have to face the town leaders when I returned to Nazareth?

Questions plagued my mind through the five-hour journey through the hills of Galilee. Seth's wife, who usually loved any excuse to talk, seemed to sense that I needed some time to myself that day. I was grateful.

Just as the sun was beginning to dip below the horizon, we reached the town where Zacharias and Elizabeth lived. Seth guided the mule cart close enough to their home that I could see Elizabeth, bending low over her garden. I slid out of the cart and grabbed the few belongings I had brought with me. As she saw me walking up the path, Elizabeth's wrinkled face lit up with a huge smile. I smiled back at her, calling her name as I ran to close the few yards that separated us. Suddenly she gasped, putting a hand on her abdomen. She looked at me, amazed.

Then, with a strong, clear voice that didn't sound like it came from an old woman, she started to speak. "Blessed are you among women, and blessed is the child you will bear!" I was stunned. How had she known? Elizabeth laughed, her joy overflowing as she captured my hands with her own. "Why have I been favored like this, the mother of my Lord coming to see *me*? As soon as I heard you coming, the baby in my womb leaped for joy." She *was* having a baby! *The angel told the truth!*

Elizabeth embraced me, kissing my cheek. Then she drew back to look at me. "Blessed is she who has believed that the Lord would fulfill his promises to her." I couldn't believe it. It was as if Elizabeth was reading my mind. But I knew it was more than that.

The Lord is here. He had guided everyone connected to the story He was shaping. He had guided me. And He would continue to lead me ... *He would fulfill His promise.* I was so full of joy, and so amazed at God's faithfulness. Words flooded my mind, and I started to sing

> My soul magnifies the Lord,
> And my spirit rejoices in God my Savior,

> For He has looked on the humble estate of His servant.
> For behold, from now on all generations will call me blessed;
> For He who is mighty has done great things for me,
> And holy is His name.
> And His mercy is for those who fear Him
> From generation to generation.
> He has shown strength with His arm;
> He has scattered the proud in the thoughts of their hearts;
> He has brought down the mighty from their thrones
> And exalted those of humble estate;
> He has filled the hungry with good things,
> And the rich He has sent away empty.
> He has helped his servant Israel,
> In remembrance of His mercy,
> As He spoke to our fathers,
> To Abraham and to his offspring forever."[2]

I wiped happy tears away as Elizabeth embraced me again. Both of us were full of joy, amazed by God's faithfulness. I was so glad to be here, to see our Lord's hand working in such a tangible way. Here, it seemed that the confusing cloud of doubt was pushed out of my mind, like a curtain being pulled back to let the light in. My worries didn't matter when I was reminded of God's power. No circumstances could keep His plan from happening.

Whatever the next season of my journey would bring, I was sure of this: my time with Elizabeth would be one of the most blessed times of my life.

---

[2] Luke 1:46-55 (ESV)

The Promise

Part Three | Sent

Those next few months with Elizabeth and Zacharias truly were some of the best months of my life. Elizabeth and I grew very close over the weeks. She was thrilled to have someone to talk to, as Zacharias had been struck dumb after the angel revealed that he would be a father after all those years of waiting. Now he had to write his words out if he wanted to talk.

Elizabeth and I wondered about everything together as we worked around the house. We talked about what it would be like to be mothers, both of us having a child for the first time. We talked about Joseph, my parents, the people in my village, and about what would happen when I went back to Nazareth. But most of all, Elizabeth told me about our Lord.

She was a daughter of Aaron, descended from a long line of men that had served God as His priests. Her own father had been a leader in their synagogue, as Zacharias was. Elizabeth's father had read to his family every night from the ancient prophecies. She had known about the new King who would come as a babe, but would grow up to be our Mighty God; our Prince of Peace. It was strange to think that this tiny child growing within me would have such power. But I knew that God had a reason for sending His Son to our humble world. This baby would grow into a strong man—a King who would lead us out from under Rome's tyranny.

Even there, in a town farther removed from Jerusalem and less traveled by the Roman soldiers, I saw the pain that our oppressors were causing as I traveled back to Nazareth. A man, bloodied and broken, hung in a tree. A woman stood nearby, sobbing as two small children clung to her skirts. A young father's life ... snuffed out.

I felt a longing in my heart, a thirst for peace and justice. I'm sure all of us did. But seeing that man reminded me of another prophecy that Elizabeth had told me of—one that put a lump in my throat every time I thought of it. My son—my gift from God Himself—would die a gruesome, awful death if the prophecy came true. He would die for sins He had never committed. And somehow, through that, He would bring us peace.

Peace ... peace from an innocent death. I thought of the prophecy again as the old mule cart bumped down the road to Nazareth. *How will this child be our King if He's dead?* If God could give His son to a virgin, why couldn't He find a way to fulfill His plan without the death of our Messiah?

I shook my head, trying to clear the doubts from my mind. The Lord knew what He was doing, even if I couldn't see His plan as clearly as I wished.

All the hours I had spent with Elizabeth talking about our God's perfect timing had done nothing to ease my unrest about Joseph. It seemed that when I had shared the angel's news, I had also given him the power to either crush me or save me. If he chose to believe me, the people would see my pregnancy as impatience; a breaking of tradition; something to be looked down on and whispered about.

But if he chose to reject me—to report to the leaders that I was pregnant with a child that was not his ... I would probably not live past the next few days. Immorality was not to be tolerated.

I blinked hard, trying to remember what it felt like to rest in God's promise. Elizabeth's first greeting seemed to have happened years earlier, rather than a mere three months ago. Now, as I got closer and closer to my hometown, I felt my heart racing. I folded my cloak around my middle, hiding the slight bump that would only get more obvious.

What are you doing, Lord? If this is Your plan? Why didn't Joseph understand?

I put a smile on my face as we pulled into the center of Nazareth. My sister ran to meet us, pulling me into a hug. Her hand lingered for half a second on my abdomen. She pulled away, and I could see in her eyes the uncertainty that filled my own mind.

"How are they?" she asked, breaking into my distracted thoughts.

"They're doing well. Elizabeth's time is very close now."

Her face lit up with a huge smile. "So you were right!" She threw her arms around me again.

"No ... the angel was right," I whispered close to her ear

"I knew it." She didn't stop smiling as we walked the half-mile to our house. I wished for that joy to come back into my own heavy heart, but I couldn't stop thinking about Joseph.

It turned out that I didn't have to wonder for long. I was just beginning to put my things away back at the house when Joseph burst through the door, slightly out of breath.

"Mary." My name caught in his throat as he jogged over to me, seeming not to notice that Leah was standing right there. Suddenly I was in his arms, my head pressed against his chest. I could hear his quick heartbeat.

He drew back, and I saw Leah tiptoe out of the room. "I just heard you returned. I had to see you."

I wasn't sure what to think. *Has he changed his mind?* I looked up at him, waiting.

"Come with me," he said, a smile pulling at the corner of his mouth. He led me to the shade of some trees by the stable, the same place where I had told Leah about the angel. We sat down together, and I pulled my scarf close around my shoulders, surprised at the nip in the autumn wind.

"You will never believe what happened while you were gone," Joseph said, his eyes shining. "The day when you came to me in town … that was the day you left to visit your relatives?"

I nodded, wondering where he was going with this. He sighed. "I wish I could have seen you again before you left. So much—" He laughed softly. "So much changed that night." Joseph turned to meet my eyes. "I was…I was wrong for not believing you."

I was surprised to feel a tear slipping down my cheek as I looked into his sincere eyes. *God? You are working in Joseph's heart, too?*

"An angel—it must have been an angel—came to me. And I'm not sure if I was dreaming, or if he was actually standing there in the doorway." I nodded again, remembering how I had felt when the angel suddenly appeared on the path. So real, but so different from ordinary men.

"I'm ashamed to say that I was thinking about breaking off our engagement." His words came out in a rush. "I was ..." He swallowed hard. "I was afraid of what might happen to me—to my reputation—if the people knew that this child was already conceived." I didn't blame him. I covered his hand with my own, waiting for him to finish.

"But then that angel came. Woke me out of a dead sleep." He stared off into the distance, remembering. "Joseph, son of David, do not be afraid to take Mary as your wife, for the child conceived in her is of the Holy Spirit. And she will bring forth a Son, and you shall call His name Jesus, for He will save His people from their sins." I could tell from the way he said it that he was repeating word for word what he had heard.

"You believed him?" I said, though I was sure of the answer.

He looked at me, his brown eyes twinkling. "He was an angel, Mary. You know how angels are."

Goose bumps raced across my arms as we laughed. My Lord of miracles was carefully paving every step of His Son's journey into the world—even changing the heart of the man who loved me.

Those next few weeks were hard, even though I knew in my heart that this was God's plan. I had seen my mother glancing at the slight bump that was my baby, and knew I wouldn't be able to hide my secret much longer. I told the rest of my family the news not long after I got back. Benjamin and my parents were unbelieving at first, even angry; afraid of what would happen to our family name, I was sure. They talked to my sister, and to Joseph, amazed that even my betrothed backed up this farfetched story I was telling them.

My mother seemed to soften towards me after a few days. She didn't talk over me when I tried my best to answer her questions, and she continued to do chores alongside me.

My father, however, was a different story. What few words we had exchanged before I had left were long gone. Now, there was only silence in the rare moments when I was alone with him. He turned his back when I walked in the room. He refused to meet my eye when we sat at dinner together. Benjamin followed his example, completely ignoring me.

The rejection from my family hurt, but Joseph decided to marry me early, heeding what the angel said about not being afraid. Together, we traveled the few miles to a synagogue in a neighboring village. The rabbi was a friend of Joseph's grandfather, but the people there didn't know us. We were married in a simple ceremony, so far from the day-long celebration that would have followed our marriage if we were free to have a normal relationship. But this baby—this gift from God—was changing everything. I was sure that this was just the first sacrifice Joseph and I would have to make.

Joseph was such a comfort to me in those days. He reminded me of the faithfulness of our God, which I tried hard not to doubt as the village whispered behind my back, some people even criticizing me to my face. Joseph and I decided to keep living apart until the baby was born, even though we were married. I was so grateful for the just man God had given me.

Five months after I got home, in the coldest part of the year, I was sitting with Leah as she worked by the fire. Everything was peaceful and quiet, the people in our village mostly keeping to themselves and trying to stay warm in their own homes.

Then, everything changed.

I heard a noise outside the window—a shout, I thought. I felt the vibrations of a hundred horse hooves pounding the frozen ground. Then they were there. Roman soldiers—many more than the usual number sent to keep an eye on our village. I heard their harsh voices shouting as they knocked down doors, demanding that everyone come to the synagogue. Leah and I called my father and Benjamin in from outside, helping Mother find her wrap and hurrying out before the soldiers could reach us.

I struggled to keep up, trying to breathe as I followed the crowd. When we reached the area in front of the synagogue, more soldiers met us. A sheen of sweat covered their horses' flanks, even in the cold. Their riders sawed at the bit, turning the beautiful animals in tight circles.

"Make a line!" Loud voices, cursing, screaming, hurting my ears. "Stupid people, make a line, is it that hard? Come on, old man." A soldier intentionally bumped our rabbi, catching him off balance. He fell hard to the ground, blood instantly pouring from a gash on his thin arm.

Before we could stop him, Benjamin was at his side. The same soldier who had pushed the old rabbi was still standing there, staring as this strong village boy mostly carried the old man back to his house. I wanted to scream. Benjamin knew better than to stand in the way of a Roman.

Tensely, I stood there with Leah and my mother, hoping against hope that the soldier would choose to let this slide.

But the soldier hoisted himself onto his horse, heavy armor clanking. He dug his heels into the poor animal's side and galloped around the corner.

I heard the screaming. Screams of a boy who was almost a man. Rebellious words flying out of his mouth unchecked, as we had always feared. I heard the soldier's whip fly, slicing through the air and landing with a sharp slap somewhere on my brother's body. I buried my face in my mother's shoulder, heartsick as I heard my brother cry out.

"He's just a boy!" Leah raised her voice over the chaos around us, and I saw several of the soldiers look at my desperate, light-haired, beautiful sister. I didn't like what I saw in their eyes.

Then Joseph's protective hand was on my hip, his thumb grazing my protruding middle. "Come on," he said over the noise, as the whip fell yet again. I could hear the clamor of the soldiers even as we reached Joseph's shop and he led me to a sleeping mat. "Rest. You'll be safe. They won't come back here." He tried to smile as he stepped back outside, shutting the door tight behind him.

I hadn't even realized how labored my breathing had become until I lay down and tried to get comfortable. But rest didn't come. I heard the soldiers' shouting even here, though the whipping seemed to have stopped.

I stayed there in Joseph's house for what felt like an eternity. Finally, I heard the noises of the soldiers leaving the village. No doubt they were leaving wreckage behind them, as the big groups of them always did.

But for me, this day was something different. I knew how cruel the Romans could be. I didn't even know if my brother was alive. I shuddered, the whip's sharp crack echoing through my head yet again.

I slowly got to my feet and made my way down the road, back to the synagogue. People talked in hushed tones, standing together in frightened clusters. They were all too aware that leftover soldiers could be quietly hidden away somewhere, listening to conversations so they could weed out the rebellious ones from among us.

I saw my mother and father clinging to each other in front of our house, and immediately my heart jumped into my throat. I moved toward them as fast as I could in my condition, questions flooding out of my mind. "What did they do? Where is Leah? Where … what happened to Benjamin? Is he—" I stopped as, at the sound of my brother's name, my mother started sobbing, her shoulders shaking uncontrollably.

"Father?" He wouldn't look at me, wouldn't respond. "Where's Benjamin? Did they … is he?" My voice trailed off. I didn't want to think about the possibility, but there it was, staring me straight in the face.

"Mary!" Joseph again appeared beside me, taking one of my hands with both of his. "Why are you back here? These soldiers, they're not safe for you to be around." I was so glad to see him. Maybe he could tell me how to understand the madness that had so quickly ripped through our village.

"Why were they here, Joseph? What could they want with us?"

He sighed deeply, his eyes dark. "Money. Caesar is enforcing a new tax. Much more severe than it has been."

Money? I could count on one hand the families in Nazareth that had money to spare. We worked hard for what we earned and hardly ever had extra. Caesar's taxes took away whatever hope we had of getting ahead. I stared at the ground, wondering how our meager earnings could carry my family through even harsher taxes.

My family. I jerked my eyes back up to meet Joseph's. "Benjamin. How is he? And why is Leah not with my mother?"

Something like a deep sadness mixed with fiery anger burned in Joseph's eyes as he stood there, finding his words. I was scared of whatever was coming. My hands shook as I pondered the possibilities. *Why can't my brother just control his tongue? And why did Leah have to draw attention to herself like that?*

Finally Joseph spoke. "Benjamin ... Benjamin is gone."

Gone. "Did he ... did they ..." I swallowed back the tears. "He is dead?"

"No." He shook his head, his jaw tight. "Worse. They saw how strong he was from his farming work. And they were afraid that he would start a rebellion if he was allowed to live on here, so ... " His words came quick, rushed. Like he was trying to speak before I could stop him. He wouldn't meet my eyes. "He's on his way to Rome. To train as a gladiator."

A gladiator. A warrior, an expert at killing other young men for the entertainment of rich Romans. Benjamin would despise it. But at least ... at least he was alive.

"And Leah?" Surely he had given me the bad news first. Leah was just tending the rabbi's wound, or helping a family repair their home.

"She—your father didn't have the money. For the taxes. And the soldier saw your sister." Joseph finally looked at me, his eyes telling me he wished he didn't have to be the one with me right then. I couldn't control my shaking. Dread wrapped itself around my heart as Joseph told me that my sister was on her way to Rome as well. To be payment for our debt. To be traded like a helpless sheep at market.

Black spots danced in front of my eyes, slowly at first, then taking over completely. I think I remember Joseph catching me in his arms. Then I must have passed out, because I woke up back in Joseph's house, blinking at too-bright sunlight streaming through the window.

"You're awake." Joseph was beside me, brushing my hair off my forehead. "I shouldn't have told you so suddenly like that. I'm sorry."

His words rushed through my mind again. *Rebellion. Rome. Payment. Leah.* I blinked hard, still trying to process that I might never see any of my siblings again. First my oldest brother Asher, years ago. And now, my little brother. And my sister—my closest friend.

I sat up, and Joseph wrapped his arms around me. "I'm so sorry," he said again, rocking me gently.

"It's not your fault," I whispered. "It's just ..." My throat closed as the reality of what he was saying wrapped its cold fingers around my heart. *My family will never be the same.*

Part Three | Sent

I tried to turn the darkness that I felt into words, but tears took over too quickly.

We stayed like that for a moment, then I pulled away, wiping my eyes. "My parents. How are they taking it?" I remembered my mother's sobs, my father's steely silence.

"They'll be alright." Joseph tried to smile. "But your father … he says you should come with me instead of staying here."

"Come with you? Where?"

He blinked a few times. "To Bethlehem. For the census. Didn't I tell you?"

I shook my head, bewildered. "No … I must have not heard you." *A census.* The emperor hadn't called for a census in years. "Is that why the soldiers were here?"

"They were here mostly for the taxes. But also to announce the census." He sighed, brushing his fingers against my waist. "They said everyone has to go to the town where they were born and register. I was born in Bethlehem."

Bethlehem. It was far, far away from Nazareth. A journey of maybe seventy miles. "But … how can they expect everyone to make such a long journey?" It would take Joseph three or four days to travel to Nazareth on his own, and I couldn't imagine how much bringing his pregnant wife would slow him down. I felt tired just thinking of walking such a distance.

Joseph's jaw tightened as he stared out the window. "I'll never understand Rome. Power-hungry; that's all they are." He made a disgusted noise, shaking his head. "Caesar must want to know how many people are under his control. That can be the only reason for a census like this. I'm sure he doesn't think of how hard it would be for the people."

Suddenly, a conversation I had had with Elizabeth flashed through my mind, and a thought hit me. *This is not just another census from a power-crazed government.* And it wasn't just my angry father that was sending me on a hard journey alongside my husband.

I grabbed Joseph's hand, finally understanding. "Bethlehem!"

He looked at me, surprised. "What?"

"The Messiah prophecy! The baby will be born in Bethlehem, remember?"[3]

The truth slowly dawned on him as he met my eyes. "Our new King ... born in little Bethlehem." He laughed softly.

The promise. Another step of the plan to carry it out was slowly making itself clear.

Lord ... this won't be easy. I silently prayed. *Give me your strength.* Our Messiah would come in Bethlehem. God would keep His word. We were safe in His hand.

Nothing will be impossible with God.

---

[3] Micah 5:2

Part Four | Given

A week after the soldiers came to Nazareth, I was riding Joseph's donkey, wrapped in a shawl against the wind. We were four days into our journey to Bethlehem, tired and chilled to the bone.

At the beginning of our trip, the journey to register in Joseph's hometown had felt like nothing more than a big adventure. We talked and laughed as Joseph led the donkey through the crowded roads.

But it only took a few hours for us to realize that this trip would be even harder than we had expected. When we stopped in a small village, Joseph left me with the donkey while he bought some food at an inn. He took only a few coins with him, leaving me with the rest. I had thought I was being watchful, but when he came back, the small pouch of coins that had been tucked into one of our sacks was nowhere to be found. Somehow, in the mass of people that surrounded me, a skillful pick pocket had stolen all the money that was supposed to provide for us on all the days of this trip.

I felt awful. The pouch had contained Joseph's savings from many weeks of hard work. Worse, now we had to face the possibility of not being able to pay for food or lodging.

But that didn't turn out to be the only thing that made me feel awful. I was quickly discovering that the back of a donkey is not the most comfortable place for a pregnant woman to sit, especially when the donkey is getting tired and tripping over everything in his path. By the end of that first day, all I wanted was a place to lie down and rest.

Of course, with the pouch gone, we didn't have the option of staying in a relatively comfortable inn. Joseph still had the change from his purchases in the village, but that was barely enough to pay for one night. We decided to save it for when we got to Bethlehem.

That night, Joseph found us a quiet place off the road, in a field that would be used for growing grain once it was planting season. Joseph slept on the stubbly, cold ground, exhausted from walking all day on the uneven, little-used roads. I tried to get comfortable and wrapped myself up in my warm cloak, but I never made it past dozing.

One long day slipped into another cold night, then another and another. Finally, we were on our fifth day of traveling.

The longer I knew Joseph, the more he seemed to be a blessing that God had personally picked out for me. Even facing the freezing cold weather, unusual for where we lived, and many, many miles in shoes that were falling apart, Joseph would turn around and smile at me once in a while. He asked if I was all right every time the donkey stumbled. I couldn't remember hearing him grumble once during that entire trip to Bethlehem.

Just before dark on that night, five days after we had left Nazareth, Bethlehem appeared on the horizon, far away in the distance. Joseph wanted to keep going, to get as close as we could before nightfall, but I was so tired. I could barely hold my head up after five long, windy days of bumpy donkey riding.

As Joseph and I stood there at the top of a hill, deciding where we would rest that night, I caught a blur of light in the valley below. I could just make out a man, a shepherd most likely, sitting by a flickering fire.

I hooked my arm around Joseph's and stared down at the man, longing for the warmth that seemed to surround the shepherd. Joseph followed my gaze, then sighed and smiled down at me resignedly, almost reading my mind. He took my hand and carefully guided me down closer to the fire, tying the donkey to a bush along the way.

"Who's there?" the man's scratchy voice called to us.

Joseph laughed, but the sound was worn out. "Two weary travelers who haven't seen a warm fire in a very long time."

The man stood up and beckoned us over. "And I haven't had company in a very long time." His smile was missing a few teeth, but was welcoming all the same. I couldn't help but smile back as my eyes wandered over his rough, plain features. His skin was toughened by weeks spent in harsh sunlight and cold wind, and there was nothing about him that was remarkable. A lamb wandered over to the warmth of the fire, and he pulled it into his lap with gentle hands.

This man was probably an outcast, like most shepherds were. My work with my neighbor's few animals had been an exception—just a way to make a few extra pennies. But most shepherds were sent away into the wilderness, often alone, to watch over huge flocks. Sometimes they spent their whole lives out in the fields, protecting the helpless. Even though his life was probably humble, his time spent on such a mind-numbing task, I could see a spark in his eyes, a hint that maybe this man would understand us. That he believed the promise, too.

The three of us sat there quietly for a few minutes. Joseph leaned forward and rubbed his hands over the fire. I leaned my head against his broad back, finally resting.

Part Four | Given

"On your way to David's city?" The shepherd broke the silence.

"Yes, actually," Joseph said, a little surprised. I held back a smile. *Where else would this path lead us?* I looked around me, at the dark, rolling hills dotted by scraggly bushes and tangles of dry grass. We were truly in the middle of nowhere.

The wonder of what was happening dawned on me once again. *Our Savior. Coming to people like us. In a place like this.* Bethlehem was obviously more populated than this quiet valley, but it was not a big city by any stretch of the imagination. Compared to where He was coming from, our world was nothing more than a dark valley. And the Lord was sending His Son here. To poor parents who barely had enough to pay Caesar's taxes.

This new King was not going to choose whom He was close to based on how much money they had. This King—my gift from God—would be a friend to even the humblest person. *Immanuel.* God would be with us. Even the lowliest of us.

I shook my head and laughed softly. Joseph looked back at me but didn't say anything. At that point he was already used to all the little things I was slowly figuring out and storing up in my heart. They were treasures to me ... little hints that God truly was fulfilling His promise. That He knew what He was doing.

The shepherd seemed to sense how bone-tired Joseph and I were, so he didn't try to make conversation. We sat together in that little haven from the cold, and I must have fallen asleep like that. Before I knew it, Joseph was gently shaking my shoulder and sunlight was peeping over the horizon. The shepherd was nowhere in sight, but just as we were heading back toward the trail, he came around a sharp turn holding a bundle out in front of him.

"Goat's cheese. And wild grapes." He pressed the bundle into my hands, smiling that gap-toothed smile yet again. Then he put his hand on my arm, his cloudy eyes meeting mine. "Your child. He is no ordinary child." He paused, looking far into the distance at a passing cloud. "I can tell he will be no ordinary child. He will bring us hope."

The way he spoke was so sure, almost prophetic. I felt a shiver run over my arms. *How could he have known?* But as I nodded, a little dazed ... I knew. God was working here. Even in this shepherd's heart.

We went on our way then. I was more rested than I had been through that whole journey. I was so grateful for the peace. Even as we grew closer to the city and had to pass through rows and rows of Roman guards, the peace stayed with me.

But then, the pains started. They came slowly at first, far enough apart that I wondered if they were real. But that didn't last long. Soon I was gritting my teeth as each pang hit me. Joseph must have heard me gasp, because as we crossed into the city limits, he turned around. His eyes were dark, concerned.

"It's time." That was all I said, but I've never seen two words have more of an effect on a man. He started walking again, rushing so fast that he was almost jogging. We had been traveling for most of the day, and shadows were getting longer and longer as the sun dipped. I couldn't even focus on the sights around me. I couldn't think about anything but finding my next breath. We stopped suddenly, crushed in a crowd of loud people. Joseph looked back at me, frantic. "I can see an inn. It won't be much longer."

He was right about one thing. *It won't be much longer.* I had never done this before, but somehow I knew that much.

It took hours to reach the inn's doors through the crowd. At least that's what it felt like. I grimaced as another pain hit me, stronger than any of the rest. Joseph looked back at me one last time, then pressed through the crowd and pounded on the door.

I saw the door open just a crack, and a man was yelling out the door. "We're full! No more room!" So many people. Of course. All the people here for the census couldn't fit in one building. A sinking, frantic feeling swelled in my chest, making it even harder to breathe.

Joseph was back at my side. "I think I see another place, Mary. We'll find something." He grabbed the donkey's head and moved as fast as he could down a side street. "We will. We'll find a place." He seemed to be talking more to himself than to me.

The donkey stopped again, and I heard Joseph knocking on a door, then another and another. "No room!" I heard the same words over and over, a little of my hope fading every time an innkeeper's voice rose over the crowd.

I cried out as an even stronger pain came over me. Joseph was picking me up off the donkey, cradling me in his strong arms. "Please! We need somewhere to stay, just one night!" He was pleading, shouting desperately to whoever could hear us. I realized the sky was dark. Night had already fallen.

Then a young woman appeared by our side, touching my arm. "Follow me."

Joseph followed her, trying not to jostle me. The girl stopped. "I'm sorry. I tried to tell everyone that we needed someone to leave so that a pregnant woman would have a place. No one would listen." She dragged her fingers through her hair, frustrated. "This is all I have." I looked down, and it took me a moment to figure out what I was looking at.

A stable. This baby would be born in a stable.

Joseph waited as the girl rushed around, shooing a few animals into a pen, forking the dirty bedding to the side and putting down fresh straw. Joseph took off his cloak and handed it to the girl. She laid it over a pile of clean straw, and Joseph lowered me down onto it. I smiled gratefully at her. The girl couldn't have been much older than I was.

A few minutes later, an older women walked into that drafty stable. My mind was cloudy at that point, but I still remember the gratefulness I felt when God provided someone who knew how to do this. She spoke softly, calmly, and told me what to do. Those were the most physically painful moments of my entire life, but when she laid my baby in my arms, I almost forgot them.

There He was. Still wet, trembling, and wailing at the top of His tiny lungs.

He was here. The Messiah.

And for now … He was mine.

I held Him close to my heart, not even knowing what to do with the incredible love for this child that was filling me to overflowing. I just couldn't stop looking at Him. His perfect eyelashes. The way His tiny red fingers curled into tight fists. The downy, dark hair that covered His little head. He was so perfect. Yet, from what I could see, He was built just like every other baby I had seen.

He wasn't just the Son of God. He was a baby. And He was my responsibility. I looked up at Joseph, and saw a little of what I was feeling in his wide eyes.

"I … I wonder if … I'll ever be able to …" He stared down at the baby. "I don't know how to hold a baby," he said with a nervous chuckle. "But He's—"

I reached over and put my free hand over his. I knew what he meant. I was a little afraid of what would happen to this baby. Actually I was more than a little afraid. How would I feel if I accidentally bumped his head while I carried him through a doorway? Or if I let Him get too close to my cooking fire and He burnt Himself? Or what if I let Him get away from me when I was at market and someone else carried Him away?

I took a deep breath, holding it in for a long time before I finally let it out. *Lord, this is Your baby. Help us.*

Help us.

I kept praying that, over and over, even as we wrapped the baby in the strips of cloth that the midwife provided. Joseph gently took Him from me and put him on a bed of straw in a feeding trough. A manger. A box that the animals usually ate out of. *Not even a real cradle to put Him in.*

I closed my tired eyes and leaned back against Joseph's cloak. I didn't understand what God was doing. This baby—this boy who would grow up to be our King—he shouldn't have to be born in a place like this. In a stable with a dirt floor. Sleeping in a feeding trough.

I was just starting to doze when a commotion made me sit up. Shadowy figures were appearing in the blackness that was the stable door. "Who's there?" Joseph said, holding the lantern up and squinting.

"We …" A rough voice tried to get words out. "Is the baby here?"

My heart skipped a beat. *How did they know?* But I knew the answer. God was here, too. He was with me the day the angel came to me. He was with my father when I was allowed to leave to see Elizabeth. He was with Elizabeth's baby. With Joseph. With that shepherd in the valley. And now …

Four or five dusty, wide-eyed men came closer to the manger, their eyes glistening in the light of the lantern. The youngest of them, a teenager with dark skin and darker hair, turned to me. "There was a man. Out in the fields with us." His voice trembled a little. "He just showed up out of nowhere. Out of the wind or something. And he had this light all around him."

One of the others laughed a little. "Scared the livin' daylights out of you."

The younger one shoved his shoulder. "And you too. Be quiet."

I smiled. I knew how angels could be. "But he told us, 'Do not be afraid, because I bring you good news. Great joy for all people. Because a Savior was born this night in David's city. He is Christ the Lord.'" He shook his head, wondering. He stared at the little sleeping bundle, my little Jesus. "He said we'd know we found the right baby when we saw Him wrapped in swaddling clothes, lying in a manger."[4]

The boy knelt down by the manger, his fingers poised in mid-air by the baby's smooth cheek. "Can I ...?"

I nodded, not caring about the dirt wedged under his fingernails or the smell of sheep on his rough clothes. This baby was a Savior. His birth was bringing—what had the angel said?—*Great joy for all the people.*

Another shepherd stepped closer, turning to gaze at the child. "Then there were more angels. I mean, they must have been angels. They filled up the whole sky. It was ..." His eyes widened, and he shook his head as he remembered, his voice trailing off. I couldn't imagine what it must have been like to see a multitude of angels. "They were singing 'Glory to God in the highest. And on earth—peace. Goodwill to men.'" He, too, knelt down next to the manger, his hands folded by his chin.

Another voice was speaking. "We left the flocks. We had to see the baby." The man stopped, his eyes welling with awestruck tears. "The Lord ... He is with us."

Then all the shepherds were on their knees, bowing to this tiny, sleeping child. My heart was so full then, even fuller

---

[4] Luke 2:10-12

than it had been when I met Elizabeth. I thought I could see why God was sending His Son to such a humble place.

Jesus was a King. But He wasn't at all like the kings we had. He was here to be a servant. He wouldn't shy away from poor people, from the ones who had nothing to offer but their worship. He was here to be a Friend to the friendless. A Rescuer of the helpless. A Savior. I hated to think of it ... but He would be our Sacrifice. A Servant who would choose to give up everything to bring us peace.

I added every one of the moments from that quiet night to the other treasures that this journey had brought me. And even after that night, when our God brought Simeon and Anna into our lives to share a little more of His plan, I kept wondering at how my Lord kept His promises. God even led the magi from far, far away in the east. They were led there by a star—a sign that only God could have managed. Those wise men covered in jewels and fine clothing bowed down before little Jesus, bringing Him precious gifts. And even later than that, God protected us from our awful, cruel government when Herod schemed to kill Jesus—when a boy was a threat to our bloodthirsty ruler.

God's fingerprints were all over His Son's life. Even when Jesus was young, I could see my Lord keeping His promise. Even when it felt like the world around us was so dark that nothing would ever work out the way God had planned it ... He never left us.

The angel's words still ring in my ears to this day:

Nothing will be impossible with God.

The Promise

Hope

I can still remember what that last night felt like.

It was my freshman year of high school. I was getting ready to perform as the pianist in my school's fall production. I was the pianist in the band—my first year getting to do something that big.

My mom helped me pick out a dress and curled my honey-brown hair for me. We laughed at how we looked, how similar, standing there next to each other in front of the mirror. Same green eyes, same heel-enhanced height.

Then there was the thrill of walking through the doors at school, realizing that opening night was finally here. All the hours of practicing, rehearsing with the cast—and now it was finally here.

I started to freak out when I realized I had forgotten my music binder in my mom's car. The conductor didn't have any spare copies. My mom had already left to get my grandpa. My phone went dead when I tried to call her.

I remember really being surprised when I saw my brother Dax by the band pit, dark hair hanging in his eyes, talking to a guy in skinny jeans. Dax was not an artsy guy. He was a guy who played basketball until one in the morning and then came back smelling like cigarettes. He never cut his hair and wore nothing but black. He loved his friends much more than the parents who didn't understand him. But he was there that night—just to watch his little sister.

I ran up to him and asked him to drive me home. *I just need five minutes to get over there and grab my music. Please, Dax. Five minutes.* He looked exasperated. But he still drove me home.

I remember how weird it felt to drive with him for the first time, though he'd had his license for more than a year. I remember how I fiddled with the radio on the way back to the school, looking for a way to fill the awkward space between us.

Then I remember a screech and headlights that were too bright. I remember Dax yelling something. I remember an awful, screaming crash.

And that was all.

When I opened my eyes, my head throbbed, and I was in a hospital room—a strange, silent hospital room. I smelled the antiseptic, saw the one tiny window with a view of a brick wall. I felt the slippery greenish gown that covered my shoulders. When I swung my feet down next to the bed, I could feel the tug of an IV line in my arm. I even felt the vibrations of a cart rolling through the hallway.

But something was missing.

I saw a pair of black high-heeled boots walking toward me. I dragged my eyes up from the floor to see my mom. She smelled like flowers and vanilla. She didn't even say hi, just sat down in the plastic, squeaky-looking chair next to me. But the chair didn't make a sound. She took one of my hands in both of hers. I finally met her eyes.

Then I realized that her lips were moving. Soundlessly. She stared at me, concerned.

Hope

"Did you say something, Mom?" I thought I was talking, felt the words slip out. But the sound was just an echoing hum.

"Mom?" I tried again. Her lips were moving again. She squeezed my hand. I watched a tear roll down the side of her nose. But still, she just mouthed whatever she was trying to say. *Why won't she just talk to me?*

Then I remembered her boots—the ones that always made so much noise when she walked on hard floors. I hadn't heard them. I didn't hear the beeping of the monitor set up next to me. I didn't hear the curtains swishing against the open window. And I couldn't hear my mom's words.

I was deaf.

The crashing noise with the too-bright headlights had come from a delivery truck flying through a red light and T-boning my brother's Jeep. My head had cracked against the window when the truck slammed into the driver's side.

I was unconscious for two full weeks ... brain-damaged.

And now ... I might never hear again.

I had already had tests, and tests, and more tests, and a surgery that left a scar along my hairline near my ear. But no one knew how to fix me.

All this I learned from the longest, most awful text message I had ever read. Spoken words didn't mean anything to me for those first few days. They just frustrated me.

My mom typed another text message when I asked about Dax.

> The truck missed the front of the jeep. Dax is still pretty banged up.

"How banged up?"

My mom stared at the blinking cursor on her screen and bit the inside of her lip. She looked up at me, and then back down again. She typed. Then she held out her phone.

> He broke his collarbone. Lots of bruises. And he messed up his right leg pretty badly. Thankfully he was wearing his seatbelt.

Dax wore his seatbelt and got out with bruises.

Bruises.

I had worn my seatbelt, too. And now ... I couldn't hear.

But then I saw the tears in my mom's eyes, saw her typing again.

> Linna...he lost his leg.

And that was the first thing that made me think, *maybe I'm not that bad off after all.*

I could still walk. I could see. I could talk. Maybe someday, somehow, my hearing would come back. Dax didn't have that. His leg wasn't coming back.

But we were both *alive.*

I finally got to go home after almost four weeks in the hospital. Home was ... different. Strange. Nothing felt the same without my hearing. Everything I remembered about home seemed to have an auditory memory attached to it, and coming back was like watching a movie on mute.

The only difference was that movies come with subtitles, and my world didn't.

It was *hard* for those first couple months. Christmas came and went, and it didn't even feel like a holiday for me. I couldn't go back to school, obviously, and that was really discouraging. Any time I had outside of catching up on assignments was mostly just spent in my room, a place that had always been quiet anyway.

Everyone tried to help. My mom brought me coffee every morning. She tried to get me to go to Target with her. One time she drove an hour both ways to buy me an original copy of *Pride and Prejudice* off Craigslist, which I loved. She tried so hard to cheer me up. Dad was at work a lot, like always, but he always talked really slow when he was home, slow enough for me to read his lips. He even brought me a book about American Sign Language, though I never got too far with it.

Even Dax started talking to me. That was new. Now, when I couldn't even hear him, he was being my big brother. Sometimes he would just sit in the same room with me—not saying anything—for hours. He let me turn subtitles on when he was watching TV. And once in a while he would ask me if I was okay.

But most of all, my best friend Brooke was there for me. She took me out to lunch and didn't care if people stared at us when I talked. She taught me how to tell the difference between *n*'s and *l*'s when I was reading her lips. She talked with me about boys, God, and movies, just like we used to. She treated me like a normal person. And I loved it.

But I still didn't feel normal. Most of my old friends never talked to me, never came to see me. I hated the sympathetic looks I caught when people looked at me at church. I missed a lot of pretty stupid things, like the scratch-scratch of my dog jumping against the front door when she heard me coming home.

Most of all, I missed my piano. I missed making music. I missed the feeling of getting a line of music perfect after practicing over and over. And I missed just playing random chords and somehow making something beautiful. Now, though, every time I glanced into the living room and saw the piano, I imagined the sound that would come out if I tried to make something beautiful. I wouldn't even be able to hear it, to sense if I was hitting an awful note. I was afraid.

Then one day, when Brooke was over, she gave me a little yellow piece of paper with "Rm. 117" written on it. *There's someone you should go see at the nursing home,* Brooke's lips said. *Might help you see things a little differently.*

So I did. I thought it was pretty random, but I still did it. I had only been in a nursing home a couple times, right before my Nana died. The first thing I noticed when I walked into the nursing home was the smell—I stopped trying to identify it after a couple seconds and just breathed through my mouth. I got lost in the halls a couple times but finally found Room 117. The door was closed. I knocked and then pushed it open a little. A woman in a power wheelchair answered the door.

Hello, she said.
I smiled. "Hi. I'm Linna."

I'm Mary. Mary had deep brown eyes, curly gray hair that had been twisted into a bun, and skin the color of creamy coffee. She looked so alive! I was a little taken aback after seeing so many half-asleep people on my way to her room. *Come on in.*

She opened the door and I was surprised again. It smelled delicious, like flowers and lemonade and furniture polish all mixed together. Her hospital bed had a bright quilt on it that looked handmade. There was a poinsettia plant and a pink candle on her dresser, an area rug that my feet sank into, and a bird feeder covered in sparrows outside her window. It almost felt like home.

Brooke told me you would come, Mary said. I could almost hear a Southern drawl in her slow words.

"How do you know Brooke?"

My granddaughter. She pointed to a framed picture of a younger version of herself, holding a little girl with long braids: the preschool version of Brooke. Now I could see how alike they were—their eyes were exactly the same. *She comes to see me often. Volunteers here.* She smiled. She had an unbelievably bright smile.

"She's told me a lot about you," I said, smiling back. "I never pictured you being in a nursing home, though. She describes you so young. I mean … you *are* young … but—"

Mary laughed. *It's all right, honey. I'm old.* She tapped her chest. *But my heart is young.*

I sat down in a chair that had an afghan draped over the back of it and folded my hands in my lap. I noticed an old phonograph in the corner. It looked like an antique. "Do you like music?"

I love music, she told me, nodding. *Back a few years ago, I was the best darn Gospel singer in all of Alabama.*

I smiled again. That explained the accent I thought I could see. *I guess I don't have much of an ear for music now, though. I just keep that old record player there to help me remember.*

The words sounded strangely familiar. "Why don't you listen to music anymore?"

I lost most of my hearing years ago. I had brain surgery. She shook her head and looked down. *The surgeon messed up during the procedure, hit a nerve. I haven't heard anything clearly since then.*

A tired looking nurse came in to check Mary's blood pressure, which gave me time to try to process that. Mary was so full of life, so fresh. She had been a great singer, had maybe even made a name for herself. And now ... she was like me.

The nurse left and Mary turned to face me again. I took a deep breath, finally coming up with something to say. "I guess Brooke probably told you ... I lost my hearing too."

She nodded. *I'm sorry.* I had heard that a lot these past few weeks, but I could tell she really meant it. *You're doing great reading my lips.*

I thought for a minute, trying to remember some of the ASL I had learned from the book my dad gave me. Then, hesitantly, I used my hands to ask her a question. *How long ... you no hear?* She smiled, and I could only imagine what my signs must have come out looking like, but I could tell she still understood.

It's okay, honey. I can read your lips just fine. And it's been almost twenty years now, I suppose.

Twenty years. And still, something like sunshine and joy mixed together was shining from this deaf woman's eyes. I swallowed hard. "How long … how long did it take you to get used to it?"

Aw, sweetie, I don't think I ever really got used to it. I did learn to accept it, though.

"How?"

Well ... I suppose my singing was the one thing I especially missed. Sometimes I would just get so full of joy that music would just pour right out of my heart and into a song.

Mary was mouthing the words so slowly, so clearly.

I stopped singing for a while after the surgery. I thought, you know, who would want to hear an old deaf lady screeching all over the scale?

She chuckled.

It took me a little while to realize, it wasn't the people I should care about. I was singing to Jesus, and as long as I threw my whole entire heart into His song, he wouldn't mind me being a little off pitch.

We sat there quiet for a minute. "So you went back to singing?"

She just smiled, took a sip of ginger ale from a plastic cup, and then started singing. At least I thought she was singing. I really wished I could hear her.

Because He lives, I can face tomorrow,
Because He lives, all fear is gone,
Because I know He holds the future,
And life is worth the living, just because He lives.

She looked at me hard when she was done.

You're a musician too, right, honey?

"Well yeah, I was."

No, she said, *putting her hand over mine. You are. You can't let this stop you. Do you have any idea the difference you could make with your music? Especially now?*

A guy with a nose ring stuck his head in the room and said something to Mary. She nodded. *I need to get down to the dining hall.* I stood up, still holding her hand.

You go out there and shine. Okay, Linna? I just looked straight into her kind eyes. For some reason my throat was all tight and I couldn't talk. She smiled and squeezed my hand.

I didn't stop thinking about her for the rest of the week.

It was a Thursday night when I finally decided to do it.

I pulled out the piano bench, flipped the cover off the keys.

And then I started to play.

It started with a simple C chord. Three notes in the middle of the piano. I knew I could get that much right. I almost heard the simple sound in my head.

I took a deep breath, moved my left hand to the piano, and tried another one. Seven notes and both hands this time, a G chord.

Then I let go.

Something popped into my head, and for the first time in five months, I let a song pour from my heart into my fingers. The first thing I played again was "Amazing Grace." I didn't know if it was right. I didn't know if it sounded good.

But it was my song. My amazing grace story.

When I looked up, my brother was at the edge of the piano, tears in his eyes. He mouthed one word.

Beautiful.

And I knew then that even if I never heard again, this was the one thing I could never give up.

Greatest Stories Ever Told
P.O. Box 307
Selmer, TN 38375

731-645-0106

admin@christian-history.org
http://www.GSETpublishing.com

Other books published by Greatest Stories Ever Told®:

Slavery During the Revolutionary War (April 2013)
The Apostles' Gospel (June 2013)
How to Make a Church Fail (July 2013)
Decoding Nicea (May 2014)

Coming Soon:

From Greatest Stories Ever Told author
PAUL F. PAVAO

Yippee, I Have Leukemia is a personal memoir chronicling Paul F. Pavao's experience with leukemia.
To get updates on the release date, visit
http://www.GSETpublishing.com/ and sign up for our newsletter!

And new GSET author
MATTHEW BRYAN

Near the end of his life on earth, Jesus told his disciples, "This gospel of the kingdom will be proclaimed in all the earth." *Forgotten Gospel* investigates every reference to the gospel of the kingdom in Scripture in order to reveal:

- The only message that the Bible calls "gospel."
- Where the Bible of Judaism specifically defined "the kingdom of God."
- How the gospel of the kingdom explains the atonement teaching of the Apostles.

"So revelatory that it's electrifying. How could we have missed this?"
~ Paul Pavao

For updates on progress, follow us at www.GSETpublishing.com.

Printed in Great Britain
by Amazon.co.uk, Ltd.,
Marston Gate.